Auguste Groner

The Case of the Registered Letter

CLASSIC PAGES

Auguste Groner

The Case of the Registered Letter

Reihe: classic pages

1. Auflage 2010 | ISBN: 978-3-86741-323-7

© Europäischer Hochschulverlag GmbH & Co KG

www.classic-pages.de

Contents

INTRODUCTION TO JOE MULLER   1

THE CASE OF THE REGISTERED
LETTER   5

INTRODUCTION TO JOE MULLER

Joseph Muller, Secret Service detective of the Imperial Austrian police, is one of the great experts in his profession. In personality he differs greatly from other famous detectives. He has neither the impressive authority of Sherlock Holmes, nor the keen brilliancy of Monsieur Lecoq. Muller is a small, slight, plain-looking man, of indefinite age, and of much humbleness of mien. A naturally retiring, modest disposition, and two external causes are the reasons for Muller's humbleness of manner, which is his chief characteristic. One cause is the fact that in early youth a miscarriage of justice gave him several years in prison, an experience which cast a stigma on his name and which made it impossible for him, for many years after, to obtain honest employment. But the world is richer, and safer, by Muller's early misfortune. For it was this experience which threw him back on his own peculiar talents for a livelihood, and drove him into the police force. Had he been able to enter any other profession, his genius might have been stunted to a mere pastime, instead of being, as now, utilised for the public good.

Then, the red tape and bureaucratic etiquette which attaches to every governmental department, puts the secret service men of the Imperial police on a par with the lower ranks of the subordinates. Muller's official rank is scarcely much higher than that of a policeman, although kings and councillors consult him and the Police Department realises to the full what a treasure it has in him. But official red tape, and his early misfortune... prevent the giving of any higher official standing to even such a genius. Born and bred to such conditions, Muller understands them, and his natural modesty of disposition asks for no outward honours, asks for nothing but an income sufficient for his simple needs, and for aid and opportunity to occupy himself in the way he most enjoys.

Joseph Muller's character is a strange mixture. The kindest-hearted man in the world, he is a human bloodhound when once the lure of the trail has caught him. He scarcely eats or sleeps when the chase is on, he does not seem to know human weakness nor fatigue, in spite of his frail body. Once put on a case his mind delves and delves until it finds a clue, then something awakes within him, a spirit akin to that which holds the bloodhound nose to trail, and he will accomplish the apparently impossible, he will track down his victim when the entire machinery of a great police department seems helpless to discover anything. The high chiefs and commissioners grant a condescending permission when Muller asks, "May I do this? ... or may I handle this case this way?" both parties knowing all the while that it is a farce, and that the department waits helpless until this humble little man saves its honour by solving some problem before which its intricate machinery has stood dazed and puzzled.

This call of the trail is something that is stronger than anything else in Muller's mentality, and now and then it brings him into conflict with the department,... or with his own better nature. Sometimes his unerring instinct discovers secrets in high places, secrets which the Police Department is bidden to hush up and leave untouched. Muller is then taken off the case, and left idle for a while if he persists in his opinion as to the true facts. And at other times, Muller's own warm heart gets him into trouble. He will track down his victim, driven by the power in his soul which is stronger than all volition; but when he has this victim in the net, he will sometimes discover him to be a much finer, better man than the other individual, whose wrong at this particular criminal's hand set in motion the machinery of justice. Several times that has happened to Muller, and each time his heart got the better of his professional instincts, of his practical common-sense, too, perhaps,... at least as far as his own advancement was concerned, and he warned the victim, defeating his own work. This peculiarity of Muller's character caused his undoing at last, his official undoing that is, and compelled his retirement from the force. But his advice is often sought unofficially by the Department, and to those who know, Muller's hand can be seen in the unravelling of many a famous case.

The following stories are but a few of the

many interesting cases that have come within the experience of this great detective. But they give a fair portrayal of Muller's peculiar method of working, his looking on himself as merely an humble member of the Department, and the comedy of his acting under "official orders" when the Department is in reality following out his directions.

THE CASE OF THE REGISTERED LETTER

"Oh, sir, save him if you can — save my poor nephew! I know he is innocent!"

The little old lady sank back in her chair, gazing up at Commissioner von Riedau with tear-dimmed eyes full of helpless appeal. The commissioner looked thoughtful. "But the case is in the hands of the local authorities, Madam," he answered gently, a strain of pity in his voice. "I don't exactly see how we could interfere."

"But they believe Albert guilty! They haven't given him a chance!"

"He cannot be sentenced without sufficient proof of his guilt."

"But the trial, the horrible trial — it will kill him — his heart is weak. I thought — I thought you might send some one — some one of your detectives — to find out the truth of the case. You must have the best people here in Vienna. Oh, my poor Albert — "

Her voice died away in a suppressed sob, and she covered her face to keep back the tears.

The commissioner pressed a bell on his desk. "Is Detective Joseph Muller anywhere about the building?" he asked of the attendant who appeared at the door.

"I think he is, sir. I saw him come in not long

ago."

"Ask him to come up to this room. Say I would like to speak to him." The attendant went out.

"I have sent for one of the best men on our force, Madam," continued the commissioner, turning back to the pathetic little figure in the chair. "We will go into this matter a little more in detail and see if it is possible for us to interfere with the work of the local, authorities in G— ."

The little old lady gave her eyes a last hasty dab with a dainty handkerchief and raised her head again, fighting for self-control. She was a quaint little figure, with soft grey hair drawn back smoothly from a gentle-featured face in which each wrinkle seemed the seal of some loving thought for others. Her bonnet and gown were of excellent material in delicate soft colours, but cut in the style of an earlier decade. The capable lines of her thin little hands showed through the fabric of her grey gloves. Her whole attitude bore the impress of one who had adventured far beyond the customary routine of her home circle, adventured out into the world in fear and trembling, impelled by the stress of a great love.

A knock was heard at the door, and a small, slight man, with a kind, smooth-shaven face, entered at the commissioner's call. "You sent for me, sir?" he asked.

"Yes, Muller, there is a matter here in which I

need your advice, your assistance, perhaps. This is Detective Muller, Miss — " (the commissioner picked up the card on his desk) "Miss Graumann. If you will tell us now, more in detail, all that you can tell us about this case, we may be able to help you."

"Oh, if you would," murmured Miss Graumann, with something more of hope in her voice. The expression of sympathetic interest on the face of the newcomer had already won her confidence for him. Her slight figure straightened up in the chair, and the two men sat down opposite her, prepared to listen to her story.

"I will tell you all I know and understand about this matter, gentlemen," she began. "My name is Babette Graumann, and I live with my nephew, Albert Graumann, engineering expert, in the village of Grunau, which is not far from the city of G— . My nephew Albert, the dearest, truest — " sobs threatened to overcome her again, but she mastered them bravely. "Albert is now in prison, accused of the murder of his friend, John Siders, in the latter's lodgings in G— ."

"Yes, that is the gist of what you have already told me," said the commissioner. "Muller, Miss Graumann believes her nephew innocent, contrary to the opinion of the local authorities in G— . She has come to ask for some one from here who could ferret out the truth of this matter. You are free now, and if we find that it can be done without offending the local authorities — "

"Who is the commissioner in charge of the case in G— ?" asked Muller.

"Commissioner Lange is his name, I believe," replied Miss Graumann.

"H'm!" Muller and the commissioner exchanged glances.

"I think we can venture to hear more of this," said the commissioner, as if in answer to their unspoken thought. "Can you give us the details now, Madam? Who is, or rather who was, this John Siders?"

"John Siders came to our village a little over a year ago," continued Miss Graumann. "He came from Chicago; he told us, although he was evidently a German by birth. He bought a nice little piece of property, not far from our home, and settled down there. He was a quiet man and made few friends, but he seemed to take to Albert and came to see us frequently. Albert had spent some years in America, in Chicago, and Siders liked to talk to him about things and people there. But one day Siders suddenly sold his property and moved to G— . Two weeks later he was found dead in his lodgings in the city, murdered, and now — now they have accused Albert of the crime."

"On what grounds? — oh, I beg your pardon, sir; I did not mean — "

"That's all right, Muller," said the commissioner. "As you may have to undertake the case, you might as well begin to do the questioning now."

"They say" — Miss Graumann's voice quavered — "they say that Albert was the last person known to have been in Siders' room; they say that it was his revolver, found in the room. That is the dreadful part of it — it was his revolver. He acknowledges it, but he did not know, until the police showed it to him, that the weapon was not in its usual place in his study. They tell me that everything speaks for his guilt, but I cannot believe it — I cannot. He says he is innocent in spite of everything. I believe him. I brought him up, sir; I was like his own mother to him. He never knew any other mother. He never lied to me, not once, when he was a little boy, and I don't believe he'd lie to me now, now that he's a man of forty-five. He says he did not kill John Siders. Oh, I know, even without his saying it, that he would not do such a thing."

"Can you tell us anything more about the murder itself?" questioned Muller gently. "Is there any possibility of suicide? Or was there a robbery?"

"They say it was no suicide, sir, and that there was a large sum of money missing. But why should Albert take any one else's money? He has money of his own, and he earns a good income besides — we have all that we need. Oh, it is some dreadful mistake! There is the newspaper account of the discovery of the body. Perhaps Mr. Muller might like to read that." She pointed to a sheet of newspaper on the desk. The commissioner handed it to Muller. It was an evening paper, dated G— , September 24th, and it gave an elaborate account, in provincial journalese, of the discovery that morning of the body of John Siders, evidently murdered, in his lodgings. The main facts to be gathered from the long-winded story were as follows:

John Siders had rented the rooms in which he met his death about ten days before, paying a month's rent in advance. The lodgings consisted of two rooms in a little house in a quiet street. It was a street of simple two-story, one and two family dwellings, occupied by artisans and small tradespeople. There were many open spaces, gardens and vacant lots in the street. The house in which Siders lodged belonged to a travelling salesman by the name of Winter. The man was away from home a great deal, and his wife, with her child and an old servant, lived in the lower part of the house, while the rooms occupied by Siders were in the upper story. Siders lived very quietly, going out frequently in the afternoon, but returning early in the evening. He had said to his landlady that he had many friends in G— . But during the time of his stay in the house he had had but one caller, a gentleman who came on the evening of the 23rd of September. The old maid had opened the door for him and showed him to Mr. Siders' rooms. She described this visitor as having a full black beard, and wearing a broad-brimmed grey felt hat. Nobody saw the man go out, for the old maid, the only person in the house at the time, had retired early. Mrs. Winter and her little girl were spending the night with the former's mother in a distant part of the city. The next morning the old servant, taking the lodger's coffee up to him at the usual hour, found him dead on the floor of his sitting-room, shot through the heart. The woman ran screaming from the house and alarmed the neighbours. A policeman at the corner heard the noise, and led the crowd up to the room where the dead man lay. It was plain to be seen that this was not a case of suicide. Everywhere were signs of a terrible struggle. The furniture was overturned, the dressing-table and the cupboard were open and their contents scattered on the floor, one of the window curtains was torn into strips, as if the victim had been trying to escape by way of the window, but had been dragged back into the room by his murderer. An overturned ink bottle on the table had spattered wide, and added to the general confusion. In the midst of the disorder lay the body of the murdered man, now cold in the rigour of death.

The police commissioner arrived soon, took possession of the rooms, and made a thorough examination of the premises. A letter found on the desk gave another proof, if such were needed, that this was not a case of suicide. This letter was in the handwriting of the dead man, and read as follows:

Dear Friend:

I appreciate greatly all the kindness shown me by yourself and your good wife. I have been more successful than I thought possible in overcoming the obstacles you know of. Therefore, I shall be very glad to join you day after to-morrow, Sunday, in the proposed excursion. I will call for you at 8 A.M. — the cab and the champagne will be my share of the trip. We'll have a jolly day and drink a glass or two to our plans for the future.

With best greetings for both of you,

Your old friend,

John

G—, Friday, Sept. 23rd.

An envelope, not yet addressed, lay beside this letter. It was clear that the man who penned these words had no thought of suicide. On the contrary, he was looking forward to a day of pleasure in the near future, and laying plans for the time to come. The murderer's bullet had pierced a heart pulsing with the joy of life.

This was the gist of the account in the evening paper. Muller read it through carefully, lingering over several points which seemed to interest him particularly. Then he turned to Miss Babette Graumann. "And then what happened?" he asked.

"Then the Police Commissioner came to Grunau and questioned my nephew. They had found out that Albert was Mr. Siders' only friend here. And late that evening the Mayor and the Commissioner came to our house with the revolver they had found in the room in G— , and they — they — " her voice trembled again, "they arrested my dear boy and took him away."

"Have you visited him in prison? What does he say about it himself?"

"He seems quite hopeless. He says that he is innocent — oh, I know he is — but everything is against him. He acknowledges that it was he who was in Mr. Siders' room the evening before the murder. He went there because Siders wrote him to come. He says he left early, and that John acted queerly. He knows they will not believe his story. This worry and anxiety will kill him. He has a serious heart trouble; he has suffered from it for years, and it has been growing steadily worse. I dare not think what this excitement may do for him." Miss Graumann broke down again and sobbed aloud. Muller laid his hands soothingly on the little old fingers that gripped the arm of the chair.

"Did your nephew send you here to ask for

help?" he inquired very gently.

"Oh, no" The old lady looked up at him through her tears. "No, he would not have done that. I'm afraid that he'll be angry if he knows that I have come. He seemed so hopeless, so dazed. I just couldn't stand it. It seemed to me that the police in G— were taking things for granted, and just sitting there waiting for an innocent man to confess, instead of looking for the real murderer, who may be gone, the Lord knows where, by now!" Miss Graumann's faded cheeks flushed a delicate pink, and she straightened up in her chair again, while her eyes snapped defiance through the tears that hung on their lashes.

A faint gleam twinkled up in Muller's eyes, and he did not look at his chief. Doctor von Riedau's own face glowed in a slowly mounting flush, and his eyes drooped in a moment of conscious embarrassment at some recollection, the sting of which was evidently made worse by Muller's presence. But Commissioner von Riedau had brains enough to acknowledge his mistakes and to learn from them. He looked across the desk at Miss Graumann. "You are right, Madam, the police have made that mistake more than once. And a man with a clear record deserves the benefit of the doubt. We will take up this case. Detective Muller will be put in charge of it. And that means, Madam, that we are giving you the very best assistance the Imperial Police Force affords."

Miss Babette Graumann did not attempt to speak. In a wave of emotion she stretched out both little hands to the detective and clasped his warmly. "Oh, thank you," she said at last. "I thank you. He's just like my own boy to me; he's all the child I ever had, you know."

"But there are difficulties in the way," continued the commissioner in a business-like tone. "The local authorities in G— have not asked for our assistance, and we are taking up the case over their heads, as it were. I shall have to leave that to Muller's diplomacy. He will come to G— and have an interview with your nephew. Then he will have to use his own judgment as to the next steps, and as to how far he may go in opposition to what has been done by the police there."

"And then I may go back home?" asked Miss Graumann. "Go home with the assurance that you will help my poor boy?"

"Yes, you may depend on us, Madam. Is there anything we can do for you here? Are you alone in the city?"

"No, thank you. There is a friend here who will take care of me. She will put me on the afternoon express back to G— ."

"It is very likely that I will take that train myself," said Muller. "If there is anything that you need on the journey, call on me."

"Oh, thank you, I will indeed! Thank you

both, gentlemen. And now good-bye, and God bless you!"

The commissioner bowed and Muller held the door open for Miss Graumann to pass out. There was silence in the room, as the two men looked after the quaint little figure slowly descending the stairs.

"A brave little woman," murmured the commissioner.

"It is not only the mother in the flesh who knows what a mother's love is," added Muller.

Next morning Joseph Muller stood in the cell of the prison in G— confronting Albert Graumann, accused of the murder of John Siders.

The detective had just come from a rather difficult interview with Commissioner Lange. But the latter, though not a brilliant man, was at least good-natured. He acknowledged the right of the accused and his family to ask for outside assistance, and agreed with Muller that it was better to have some one in the official service brought in, rather than a private detective whose work, in its eventual results, might bring shame on the police. Muller explained that Miss Graumann did not want her nephew to know that it was she who had asked for aid in his behalf, and that it could only redound to his, Lange's, credit if it were understood that he had sent to Vienna for expert assistance in this case. It would be a proof of his conscientious attention to duty, and would insure praise for him, whichever way the case turned out. Commissioner Lange saw the force of this argument, and finally gave Muller permission to handle the case as he thought best, rather relieved than otherwise for his own part. The detective's next errand was to the prison, where he now stood looking up into the deep-set, dark eyes of a tall, broad-shouldered, black-bearded man, who had arisen from the cot at his entrance. Albert Graumann had a strong, self-reliant face and bearing. His natural expression was somewhat hard and stern, but it was the expression of a man of integrity and responsibility. Muller had already made some inquiries as to the prisoner's reputation and business standing in the community, and all that he had heard was favourable. A certain hardness and lack of amiability in Graumann's nature made it difficult for him to win the hearts of others, but although he was not generally loved, he was universally respected. Through the signs of nagging fear, sorrow, and ill-health, printed clearly on the face before him, Muller's keen eyes looked down into the soul of a man who might be overbearing, pitiless even, if occasion demanded, but who would not murder — at least not for the sake of gain. This last possibility Muller had dismissed from his mind, even before he saw the prisoner. The man's reputation was sufficient to make the thought ridiculous. But he had not made up his mind whether it might not be a case of a murder after a quarrel. Now he began to doubt even this when he looked into the intelligent, harsh-featured face of the man in the cell. But Muller had the gift of putting aside his own convictions, when he wanted his mind clear to consider evidence before him.

Graumann had risen from his sitting position when he saw a stranger. His heavy brows drew down over his, eyes, but he waited for the other to speak.

"I am Detective Joseph Muller, from Vienna," began the newcomer, when he had seen that the prisoner did not intend to start the conversation.

"Have you come to question me again?" asked Graumann wearily. "I can say no more than I have already said to the Police Commissioner. And no amount of cross-examination can make me confess a crime of which I am not guilty — no matter what evidence there may be against me." The prisoner's voice was hard and determined in spite of its note of physical and mental weariness.

"I have not come to extort a confession from you, Mr. Graumann," Muller replied gently, "but to help you establish your innocence, if it be possible."

A wave of colour flooded the prisoner's cheek. He gasped, pressed his hand to his heart, and dropped down on his cot. "Pardon me," he said finally, hesitating like a man who is fighting for breath. "My heart is weak; any excitement upsets me. You mean that the authorities are not convinced of my guilt, in spite of the evidence?

You mean that they will give me the benefit of the doubt — that they will give me a chance for life?"

"Yes, that is the reason for my coming here. I am to take this case in hand. If you will talk freely to me, Mr. Graumann, I may be able to help you. I have seen too many mistakes of justice because of circumstantial evidence to lay any too great stress upon it. I have waited to hear your side of the story from yourself. I did not want to hear it from others. Will you tell it to me now? No, do not move, I will get the stool myself."

Graumaun sat back on the cot, his head resting against the wall. His eyes had closed while Muller was speaking, but his quieter breathing showed that he was mastering the physical attack which had so shaken him at the first glimpse of hope. He opened his eyes now and looked at Muller steadily for a moment. Then he said: "Yes, I will tell you: my life and my work have taught me to gauge men. I will tell you everything I know about this sad affair. I will tell you the absolute truth, and I think you will believe me."

"I will believe you," said Muller simply.

"You know the details of the murder, of course, and why I was arrested?"

"You were arrested because you were the last person seen in the company of the murdered man?"

"Exactly. Then I may go back and tell you

something of my connection with John Siders?"

"It would be the very best thing to do."

"I live in Grunau, as you doubtless know, and am the engineering expert of large machine works there. My father before me held an important position in the factory, and my family have always lived in Grunau. I have traveled a great deal myself. I am forty-five years old, a childless widower, and live with my old aunt, Miss Babette Graumann, and my ward, Miss Eleonora Roemer, a young lady of twenty-two." Muller looked up with a slight start of surprise, but did not say anything. Graumann continued:

"A little over a year ago, John Siders, who signed himself as coming from Chicago, bought a piece of property in our town and came to live there. I made his acquaintance in the cafe and he seemed to take a fancy to me. I also had spent several years in Chicago, and we naturally came to speak of the place. We discovered that we had several mutual acquaintances there, and enjoyed talking over the old times. Otherwise I did not take particularly to the man, and as I came to know him better I noticed that he never mentioned that part of his life which lay back of the years in Chicago. I asked a casual question once or twice as to his home and family, but he evaded me every time, and would not give a direct answer. He was evidently a German by birth and education, a man with university training, and one who knew life thoroughly. He had delightful manners, and when he could forget his shyness for a while, he could be very agreeable. The ladies of my family came to like him, and encouraged him to call frequently. Then the thing happened that I should not have believed possible. My ward, Miss Roemer, a quiet, reserved girl, fell in love with this man about whom none of us knew anything, a man with a past of which he did not care to speak.

"I was not in any way satisfied with the match, and they seemed to realise it. For Siders managed to persuade the girl to a secret engagement. I discovered it a month or two ago, and it made me very angry. I did not let them see how badly I felt, but I warned Lora not to have too much to do with the boy, and I set about finding out something regarding his earlier life. It was my duty to do this, as I was the girl's guardian. She has no other relative living, and no one to turn to except my aunt and myself. I wrote to Mr. Richard Tressider in Chicago, the owner of the factory in which I had been employed while there. John had told me that Tressider had been his client during the four years in which he practiced law in Chicago. I received an answer about the middle of August. Mr. Tressider had been able to find out only that John was born in the town of Hartberg in a certain year. This was enough. I took leave of absence for a few days and went to Hartberg, which, as you know, is about 140 miles from here. Three days later I knew all that I wanted to know. John Siders was not the man's real name, or, rather, it was only part of his name. His full name was Theodor John Bellmann, and his mother was an Englishwoman whose maiden name was Siders. His father was a county official who died at an early age, leaving his widow and the boy in deepest poverty. Mrs. Bellmann moved to G— to give music lessons. Theodor went to school there, then finally to college, and was an excellent pupil everywhere. But one day it was discovered that he had been stealing money from the banker in whose house he was serving as private tutor to the latter's sons. A large sum of money was missing, and every evidence pointed to young Bellmann as the thief. He denied strenuously that he was guilty, but the District Judge (it was the present Prosecuting Attorney Schmidt in G—) sentenced him. He spent eight months in prison, during which time his mother died of grief at the disgrace. There must have been something good in the boy, for he had never forgotten that it was his guilt that struck down his only relative, the mother who had worked so hard for him. He had atoned for this crime of his youth, and during the years that have passed since then, he had been an honest, upright man."

Graumann paused a moment and pressed his hand to his heart again. His voice had grown weaker, and he breathed hard. Finally he continued: "I commanded my ward to break off her engagement, as I could not allow her to marry a man who was a freed convict. Siders sold his property some few weeks after that and moved to G— . Eleonora acquiesced in my commands, but she was very unhappy and allowed me to see very little of her. Then came the events of the evening of September 23rd, the events which have turned out so terribly. I will try to tell you the story just as it happened, so far as I am concerned. I had seen nothing of John since he left this town. He had made several attempts before his departure for G— to change my opinion, and my decision as to his marriage to my ward. But I let him see plainly that it was impossible for him to enter our family with such a past behind him. He asserted his innocence of the charges against him, and declared that he had been unjustly accused and imprisoned. I am afraid that I was hard towards him. I begin to understand now, as I never thought I should, what it means to be accused of crime. I begin to realise that it is possible for every evidence to point to a man who is absolutely innocent of the deed in question. I begin to think now that John may have been right, that possibly he also may have been accused and sentenced on circumstantial evidence alone. I have thought much, and I have learned much in these terrible days."

The prisoner paused again and sat brooding, his eyes looking out into space. Muller respected his suffering and sat in equal silence, until Graumann raised his eyes to his again. "Then came the evening of the 23rd of September?"

"Yes, that evening — it's all like a dream to me." Graumann began again. "John wrote me a letter asking me to come to see him on that evening. I tore up the letter and threw it away — or perhaps, yes, I remember now, I did not wish Eleonora to see that he had written me. He asked me to come to see him, as he had something to say to me, something of the greatest importance for us both. He asked me not to mention to any one that I was to see him, as it would be wiser no one should know that we were still in communication with each other. There was a strain of nervous excitement visible in his letter. I thought it better to go and see him as he requested; I felt that I owed him some little reparation for having denied him the great wish of his heart. It was my duty to make up to him in other ways for what I had felt obliged to do. I knew him for a nervous, high-strung man, overwrought by brooding for years on what he called his wrongs, and I did not know what he might do if I refused his request. It was not of myself I thought in this connection, but of the girl at home who looked to me for protection.

"I had no fear for myself; it never occurred to me to think of taking a weapon with me. How my revolver — and it is undoubtedly my revolver, for there was a peculiar break in the silver ornamentation on the handle which is easily recognisable — how this revolver of mine got into his room, is more than I can say. Until the Police Commissioner showed it to me two or three days ago, I had no idea that it was not in the box in my study where it is ordinarily kept." Graumann paused again and looked about him as if searching for something. He rose and poured himself out a glass of water. "Let me put some of this in it," said Muller. "It will do you good." From a flask in his pocket he poured a few drops of brandy into the water. Graumann drank it and nodded gratefully. Then he took up his story again.

"I never discovered why Siders had sent for me. When I arrived at the appointed time I found the door of the house closed. I was obliged to ring several times before an old servant opened the door. She seemed surprised that it had been locked. She said that the door was always unlatched, and that Mr. Siders himself must have closed it, contrary to all custom, for she had not done it, and there was no one else in the house but the two of them. Siders was waiting for me at the top of the stairs, calling down a noisy welcome.

"When I asked him finally what it was so important that he wanted to say to me, he evaded me and continued to chatter on about commonplace things. Finally I insisted upon knowing why he had wanted me to come, and he replied that the reason for it had already been fulfilled, that he had nothing more to say, and that I could go as soon as I wanted to. He appeared quite calm, but he must have been very nervous. For as I stood by the desk, telling him what I thought of his actions, he moved his hand hastily among the papers there and upset the ink stand. I jumped back, but not before I had received several large spots of ink on my trousers. He was profuse in his apologies for the accident, and tried to take out the spots with blotting paper. Then at last, when I insisted upon going, he looked out to see whether there was still a light on the stairs, and led me down to the door himself, standing there for some time looking after me.

"I was slightly alarmed as well as angry at his actions. I believe that he could not have been quite in his right mind, that the strain of nervousness which was apparent in his nature had really made him ill. For I remember several peculiar incidents of my visit to him. One of these was that he almost insisted upon my taking away with me, ostensibly to take care of them, several valuable pieces of jewelry which he possessed. He seemed almost offended when I refused to do anything of the kind. Then, as I parted from him at the door, not in a very good humour I will acknowledge, he said to me: 'You will think of me very often in the future — more often than you would believe now!'

"This is all the truth, and nothing but the truth, about my visit to John Siders on the evening of September 23rd. As it had been his wish I said nothing to the ladies at home, or to any one else about the occurrence. And as I have told you, I destroyed his letter asking me to come to him.

"The following day about noon, the Commissioner of Police from G— called at my office in the factory, and informed me bluntly that John Siders had been found shot dead in his lodgings that morning. I was naturally shocked, as one would be at such news, in spite of the fact that I had parted from the man in anger, and that I had no reason to be particularly fond of him. What shocked me most of all was the sudden thought that John had taken his own life. It was a perfectly natural thought when I considered his nervousness, and his peculiar actions of the evening before. I believe I exclaimed, 'It was a suicide!' almost without realising that I was doing so. The commissioner looked at me sharply and said that suicide was out of the question, that it was an evident case of murder. He questioned me as to Siders' affairs, of which I told only what every one here in the village knew. I did not consider it incumbent upon me to disclose to the police the disgrace of the man's early life. I had been obliged to hurt him cruelly enough because of that, and I saw no necessity for blackening his name, now that he was dead. Also, as according to what the commissioner said, it was a case of murder for robbery, I did not wish to go into any details of our connection with Siders that would cause the name of my ward to be mentioned. After a few more questions the commissioner left me. I was busy all the afternoon, and did not return to my home until later than usual. I found my aunt somewhat worried because Miss Roemer had left the house immediately after our early dinner, and had not yet returned. We both knew the girl to be still grieving over her broken engagement, and we dreaded the effect this last dreadful news might have on her. We supposed, however, that she had gone to spend the afternoon with a friend, and were rather glad to be spared the necessity of telling her at once what had happened. I had scarcely finished my supper, when the door bell rang, and to my astonishment the Mayor of Grunau was announced, accompanied by the same Police Commissioner who had visited me in my office that morning. The Mayor was an old friend of mine and his deeply grave face showed me that something serious had occurred. It was indeed serious! and for some minutes I could not grasp the meaning of the commissioner's questions. Finally I realised with a tremendous shock that I — I myself was under suspicion of the murder of John Siders. The description given by the old servant of the man who had visited Siders the evening before, the very clothes that I wore, my hat and the trousers spotted by the purple ink, led to my identification as this mysterious visitor. The servant had let me in but she had not seen me go out.

"Then I discovered — when confronted suddenly with my own revolver which had been found on the floor of the room, some distance from the body of the dead man, that this same revolver had been identified as mine by my ward, Eleonora Roemer, who had been to the police station at G— in the early afternoon hours. Some impulse of loyalty to her dead lover, some foolish feminine fear that I might have spoken against him in my earlier interviews with the commissioner had driven the girl to this step. A few questions sufficed to draw from her the story of her secret engagement, of its ending, and of my quarrel with John. I will say for her that I am certain she did not realise that all these things were calculated to cast suspicion on me. The poor girl is too unused to the ways of police courts, to the devious ways of the law, to realise what she was doing. The sight of my revolver broke her down completely and she acknowledged that it was mine. That is all. Except that I was arrested and brought here as you see. I told the commissioner the story of my visit to John Siders exactly as I told it to you, but it was plain to be seen that he did not believe me. It is plain to be seen also, that he is firmly convinced of my guilt and that he is greatly satisfied with himself at having traced the criminal so soon."

"And yet he was not quite satisfied," said Muller gently. "You see that he has sent to the Capital for assistance on the case." Muller felt this little untruth to be justified for the sake of the honour of the police force.

"Yes, I'm surprised at that," said Graumann in his former tone of weariness. "What do you think you will be able to do about it?"

"I must ask questions here and there before I

can form a plan of campaign," replied Muller. "What do you think about it yourself? Who do you think killed Siders?"

"How can I know who it was? I only know it is not I," answered Graumann.

"Did he have any enemies?"

"No, none that I knew of, and he had few friends either."

"You knew there was a sum of money missing from his rooms?"

"Yes, the sum they named to me was just about the price that he had received for the sale of his property here. They did me the honour to believe that if I had taken the money at all, I had done so merely as a blind. At least they did not take me for a thief as well as a murderer. If the money is really missing, it was for its sake he was murdered I suppose."

"Yes, that would be natural," said Muller. "And you know nothing of any other relations or connections that the man may have had? Anything that might give us a clue to the truth?"

"No, nothing. He stood so alone here, as far as I knew. Of course, as I told you, his actions of the evening before having been so peculiar — and as I knew that he was not in the happiest frame of mind — I naturally thought of suicide at once, when they told me that he had been found shot dead. Then they told me that the appearance of the room and many other things, proved suicide to have been out of the question. I know nothing more about it. I cannot think any more about it. I know only that I am here in danger of being sentenced for the crime that I never committed — that is enough to keep any man's mind busy." He leaned back with an intense fatigue in every line of his face and figure.

Muller rose from his seat. "I am afraid I have tired you, Mr. Graumann," he said, "but it was necessary that I should know all that you had to tell me. Try and rest a little now and meanwhile be assured that I am doing all I can to find out the truth of this matter. As far as I can tell now I do not believe that you have killed John Siders. But I must find some further proofs that will convince others as well as myself. If it is of any comfort to you, I can tell you that during a long career as police detective I have been most astonishingly fortunate in the cases I have undertaken. I am hoping that my usual good luck will follow me here also. I am hoping it for your sake."

The man on the cot took the hand the detective offered him and pressed it firmly. "You will let me know as soon as you have found anything — anything that gives me hope?"

"I will indeed. And now save your strength and do not worry. I will help you if it is in my power."

After leaving the prison, Muller took the

train for the village of Grunau, about half an hour distant from the city. He found his way easily to Graumann's home, an attractive old house set in a large garden amid groups of beautiful old trees. When he sent up his card to Miss Graumann, the old lady tripped down stairs in a flutter of excitement.

"Did you see him?" she asked. "You have been to the prison? What do you think? How does he seem?"

"He seems calm to-day," replied Muller, "although the confinement and the anxiety are evidently wearing on him."

"And you heard his story? And you believe him innocent?"

"I am inclined to do so. But there is more yet for me to investigate in this matter. It is certainly not as simple as the police here seem to believe. May I speak to your ward, Miss Roemer? She is at home now?"

"Yes, Lora is at home. If you will wait here a moment I will send her in."

Muller paced up and down the large sunny room, casting a glance over the handsome old pieces of furniture and the family portraits on the wall. It was evidently the home of generations of well-to-do, well-bred people, the narrow circle of whose life was made rich by congenial duties and a comfortable feeling of their standing in the community.

While he was studying one of the portraits more carefully, he became aware that there was some one in the room. He turned and saw a tall blond girl standing by the door. She had entered so softly that even Muller's quick ear had not heard the opening of the door.

"Do you wish to speak to me?" she said, coming down into the room. "I am Eleonora Roemer"

Her face, which could be called handsome in its even regularity of feature and delicate skin, was very pale now, and around her eyes were dark rings that spoke of sleepless nights. Grief and mental shock were preying upon this girl's mind. "She is not the one to make a confidant of those around her," thought Muller to himself. Then he added aloud: "If it does not distress you too much to talk about this sad affair, I will be very grateful if you will answer a few questions."

"I will tell you whatever I can," said the girl in the same low even tone in which she had first spoken. "Miss Graumann tells me that you have come from Vienna to take up this case. It is only natural that we should want to give you every assistance in our power."

"What is your opinion about it?" was Muller's next remark, made rather suddenly after a moment's pause.

The directness of the question seemed to

shake the girl out of her enforced calm. A slow flush mounted into her pale cheeks and then died away, again leaving them whiter than before. "I do not know — oh, I do not know what to believe."

"But you do not think Mr. Graumann capable of such a crime, do you?"

"Not of the robbery, of course not; that would be absurd! But has it been clearly proven that there is a robbery? Might it not have been — might they not have — "

"You mean, might they not have quarreled? Of course there is that possibility. And that is why I wanted to speak to you. You are the one person who could possibly throw light on this subject. Was there any other reason beyond the dead man's past that would render your guardian unwilling to have you marry him?"

Again the slow flush mounted to Eleonora Roemer's cheeks and her head drooped.

"I fear it may be painful for you to answer this," said Muller gently, "and yet I must insist on it in the interest of justice."

"He — my guardian — wished to marry me himself," the girl's words came slowly and painfully.

Muller drew in his breath so sharply that it was almost like a whistle. "He did not tell me that; it might make a difference."

"That... that is... what I fear," said the girl, her eyes looking keenly into those of the man who sat opposite. "And then, it was his revolver."

"Then you do believe him guilty?"

"It would be horrible, horrible — and yet I do not know what to think."

There was silence in the room for a moment. Miss Roemer's head drooped again and her hands twisted nervously in her lap. Muller's brain was very busy with this new phase of the problem. Finally he spoke.

"Let us dismiss this side of the question and talk of another phase of it, a phase of which it is necessary for me to know something. You would naturally be the person nearest the dead man, the one, the only one, perhaps, to whom he had given his confidence. Do you know of any enemies he might have had in the city?"

"No, I do not know of any enemies, or even of any friends he had there. When the terrible thing happened that clouded his past, when he had regained his freedom, after his term of imprisonment, there was no one left whom he cared to see again. He does not seem to have borne any malice towards the banker who accused him of the theft. The evidence was so strong against him that he felt the suspicion was justified. But there was hatred in his heart for one man, for the Justice who sentenced him, Justice Schmidt, who is now Attorney General in G— ."

"The man who, in the name of the State, will conduct this case?" asked Muller quickly.

"Yes, I believe it is so. Is it not an irony that this man, the only one whom John really hated, should be the one to avenge him now?"

"H'm! yes. But did you know of any friends in G— ?"

"No, none at all."

"No friends whom he might have made while he was in America and then met again in Germany?"

"No, he never spoke of any such to me. He told me that he made few friends. He did not seek them for he was afraid that they might find out what had happened and turn from him. He was morbidly sensitive and could not bear the disappointment."

"Why did he return to Germany?"

"He was lonely and wanted to come home again. He had made money in America — John was very clever and highly educated — but his heart longed for his own tongue and his own people."

Muller took a folded piece of paper from his pocket. "Do you know this handwriting?"

Miss Roemer read the few lines hastily and her voice trembled as she said: "This is John's handwriting. I know it well. This is the letter that was found on the table?"

"Yes, this letter appears to be the last he had written in life. Do you know to whom it could have been written? The envelope, as I suppose you know from the newspaper reports, was not addressed. Do you know of any friends with whom he could have been on terms of sufficient intimacy to write such a letter? Do you know what these plans for the future could have been? It would certainly be natural that he should have spoken to you first about them."

"No; I cannot understand this letter at all," replied the girl. "I have thought of it frequently these terrible days. I have wondered why it was that if he had friends in the city, he did not speak to me of them. He repeatedly told me that he had no friends there at all, that his life should begin anew after we were married."

"And did he have any particular plans, in a business way, perhaps?"

"No; he had a comfortable little income and need have no fear for the future. John was, of course, too young a man to settle down and do nothing. But the only definite plans he had made were that we should travel a little at first, and then he would look about him for a congenial occupation. I always thought it likely he would resume a law practice somewhere. I cannot understand in the slightest what the plans are to which the letter referred."

"And do you think, from what you know of his state of mind when you saw him last, that he would be likely so soon to be planning pleasures like this?"

"No, no indeed! John was terribly crushed when my guardian insisted on breaking off our engagement. Until my twenty-fourth birthday I am still bound to do as my guardian says, you know. John's life and early misfortune made him, as I have already said, morbidly sensitive and the thought that it would be a bar to anything we might plan in the future, had rendered him so depressed that — and it was not the least of my anxieties and my troubles — that I feared... I feared anything might happen."

"You feared he might take his own life, do you mean?"

"Yes, yes, that is what I feared. But is it not terrible to think that he should have died this way — by the hand of a murderer?"

"H'm! And you cannot remember any possible friend he may have found — some schoolboy friend of his youth, perhaps, with whom he had again struck up an acquaintance."

"Oh, no, no, I am positive of that. John could not bear to hear the names even of the people he had known before his misfortune. Still, I do remember his once having spoken of a man, a German he had met in Chicago and rather taken a fancy to, and who had also returned to Germany."

"Could this possibly have been the man to whom the letter is addressed?"

"No, no. This friend of John's was not married; I remember his saying that. And he lived in Germany somewhere — let me think — yes, in Frankfort-on-Main."

"And do you remember the man's name?"

"No, I cannot, I am sorry to say. John only mentioned it once. It was only by a great effort that I could remember the incident at all."

"And has it not struck you as rather peculiar that this friend, the one to whom the cordial letter was addressed, did not come forward and make his identity known? G— is a city, it is true, but it is not a very large city, and any man being on terms of intimate acquaintance with one who was murdered would be apt to come forward in the hope of throwing some light on the mystery."

"Why, yes, I had not thought of that. It is peculiar, is it not? But some people are so foolishly afraid of having anything to do with the police, you know."

"That is very true, Miss Roemer. Still it is a queer incident and something that I must look into."

"What do you believe?" asked the girl tensely.

"I am not in a position to say as yet. When I am, I will come to you and tell you."

"Then you do not think that my guardian killed John — that there was a quarrel between the men?"

"There is, of course, a possibility that it may have been so. You know your guardian better than I do, naturally. Our knowledge of a man's character is often a far better guide than any circumstantial evidence."

"My guardian is a man of the greatest uprightness of character. But he can be very hard and pitiless sometimes. And he has a violent temper which his weak heart has forced him to keep in control of late years."

"All this speaks for the possibility that there may have been a quarrel ending in the fatal shot. But what I want to know from you is this — do you think it possible, that, this having happened, Albert Graumann would not have been the first to confess his unpremeditated crime? Is not this the most likely thing for a man of his character to do? Would he so stubbornly deny it, if it had happened?"

The girl started. "I had not thought of that! Why, why, of course, he might have killed John in a moment of temper, but he was never a man to conceal a fault. He is as pitiless towards his own weakness, as towards that of others. You are right, oh, you must be right. Oh, if you could take this awful fear from my heart! Even my grief for John would be easier to bear then."

Muller rose from his chair. "I think I can promise you that this load will be lifted from your heart, Miss Roemer."

"Then you believe — that it was just a case of murder for robbery? For the money? And John had some valuable jewelry, I know that."

"I do not know yet," replied Muller slowly, "but I will find out, I generally do."

"Oh, to think that I should have done that poor man such an injustice! It is terrible, terrible! This house has been ghastly these days. His poor aunt knows that he is innocent — she could never believe otherwise — she has felt the hideous suspicion in my mind — it has made her suffering worse — will they ever forgive me?"

"Her joy, if I can free her nephew, will make her forget everything. Go to her now, Miss Roemer, comfort her with the assurance that you also believe him to be innocent. I must hasten back to G— and go on with this quest."

The girl stood at the doorway shaded by the overhanging branches of two great trees, looking down the street after the slight figure of the detective. "Oh, it is all easier to hear, hard as it is, easier now that this horrible suspicion has gone from my mind — why did I not think of that before?"

Alone in the corner of the smoking compartment in the train to G—, Muller arranged in his mind the facts he had already gathered. He had questioned the servants of John Siders' former household, had found that the dead man received very few letters, only an occasional business communication from his bank. Of the few others, the servants knew nothing except that he had always thrown the envelopes carelessly in the waste paper basket and had never seemed to have any correspondence which he cared to conceal. No friend from elsewhere had ever visited him in Grunau, and he had made few friends there except the Graumann family.

The facts of the case, as he knew them now, were such as to make it extremely doubtful that Graumann was the murderer. Muller himself had been inclined to believe in the possibility of a quarrel between the two men, particularly when he had heard that Graumann himself was in love with his handsome ward. But the second thought that came to him then, impelled by the unerring instinct that so often guided him to the truth, was the assurance that in a case of this kind, in a case of a quarrel terminating fatally, a man like Albert Graumann would be the very first to give himself up to the police and to tell the facts of the case. Albert Graumann was a man of honour and unimpeachable integrity. Such a man would not persist in a foolish denial of the deed which he had committed in a moment of temper. There would be nothing to gain from it, and his own conscience would be his severest judge. "The disorder in the room?" thought Muller. "It'll be too late for that now. I suppose they have rearranged the place. I can only go by what the local detectives have seen, by the police reports. But I do not understand this extreme disorder. There is no reason why there should be a struggle when the robber was armed with a pistol. If Siders was supposed to have been interrupted when writing a letter, interrupted by a thief come with intent to steal, a thief armed with a revolver, the sight of this weapon alone would be sufficient to insure his not moving from his seat. I can understand the open drawers and cupboard; that is explained by the thief's hasty search for booty. But the torn window curtain and the overturned chairs are peculiar.

"Of course there is always a possibility that the thief might have entered one room while Siders was in the other; that the latter might have surprised the robber in his search for money or valuables, and that there might have been a hand-to-hand struggle before the intruder could pull out his revolver. Oh, if I could only have seen the body! This is working under terrific difficulties. The marks of a hand-to-hand struggle would have been very plain on the clothes and on the person of the murdered man. But this letter? I do not understand this letter at all. It is the dead man's handwriting, that we know, but why did not the friend to whom it was addressed come forward and make himself known? As far as I can learn from the police reports in G— , there was no personal interest shown, no personal inquiries made about the dead man. There was only the natural excitement that a murder would create. Now a family, expecting to make a pleasure excursion with a friend in a day or two and suddenly hearing that this friend had been found murdered in his lodgings, would be inclined to take some little personal interest in the matter. These people must have been in town and at home, for the excursion spoken of in the letter was to occur two days after the murder. Miss Roemer's remark about the dread that some people have as to any connection with the police, is true to a limited extent only. It is true only of the ignorant mind, not of a man presumably well-to-do and properly educated. I do not understand why the man to whom this letter was addressed has not made himself known. The only explanation is — that there was no such man!" A sudden sharp whistle broke from the detective's lips.

"I must examine the dead man's personal effects, his baggage, his papers; there may be something there. His queer letter to Graumann — his desire that the latter's visit should be kept secret — a visit which apparently had no cause at all, except to get Graumann to the house, to get him to the house in a way that he should be seen coming, but should not be seen going away. What does this mean?

"Graumann was the only person against whom Siders had an active cause of quarrel for the moment. There was one other man whom he hated, and this other man was the prosecuting attorney who would conduct any case of murder that came up in the town of G—.

"Now John Siders is found murdered — is found killed, in his lodgings, the morning after he has arranged things so that his antagonist, his rival in love, Albert Graumann, shall come under suspicion of having murdered him.

"What evidence have we that this man did not commit suicide? We have the evidence of the disorder in the room, a disorder that could have been made just as well by the man himself before he ended his own life. We have the evidence of a letter to some unknown, making plans for pleasure during the next days, and speaking of further plans, presumably concerning business, for the future. In a town the size of G—, where every one must have read of the murder, no one has come forward claiming to be the friend for whom this letter was written. Until this Unknown makes himself known, the letter as an evidence points rather to premeditated suicide than to the contrary. Oh, if I could only have seen the body! They tell me the pistol was found some little distance from the body. Is it at all likely that a murderer would go away leaving such evidence behind him? If Graumaun had killed Siders in a hasty quarrel, he might possibly, in his excitement, have left his revolver. But I have already disposed of this possibility. A man of sufficient brains to so carefully plan his suicide as to conceal every trace of it and cast suspicion upon the man who had made him unhappy, such a one would be quite clever enough to throw the pistol far away from his body and to leave no traces of powder on his coat or any such other evidence.

"If I were to say now what I think, I would say that John Siders deliberately took his own life and planned it in such a way as to cast suspicion upon Albert Graumann. But that would indeed be a terrible revenge. And I must have some tangible proof of it before any court will accept my belief. This proof must be hidden somewhere. The thing for me to do is to find it."

The evidence gathered at the time of the death went to show that Siders had been paid a considerable sum in cash for the sale of his property at Grunau. And there was no trace of his having deposited this sum in any bank in G— or in Grunau, in both of which places he had deposited other securities. Therefore the money had presumably been in his room at the time of his death. A search had been made for this money in every possible place of concealment among the dead man's belongings, and it had not been found. Muller asked the Police Commissioner to give him the key to the rooms, which were still officially closed, and also the keys to the dead man's pieces of baggage. Commissioner Lange seemed to think all this extra search quite unnecessary, as it did not occur to him that anything else was to be looked for except the money.

It was quite late when Muller began his examination of the dead man's effects. He was struck by the fact that there was scarcely a bit of paper to be found anywhere, no letters, no business papers, except bank books showing the amount of his securities in the bank in G— and in Grunau, and giving facts about some investments in Chicago. There was nothing of more recent date and no personal correspondence whatever. The same was true of the pockets of the suit Siders had been wearing at the time of his death. A man of any property or position at all in the world gathers about him so much of this kind of material that its absence shows premeditation. The suit Siders had been wearing when he was killed was lying on the table in the room. It was a plain grey business suit of good cut and material. The body had been prepared for burial in a beseeming suit of black. Muller made a careful examination of the clothes, and found only what the police reports showed him had already been found by the examination made by the local authorities. Upon a second careful examination, however, he found that in one of the vest pockets there was a little extra pocket, like a change pocket, and in it he found a crumpled piece of paper. He took it out, smoothed and read it. It was a post office receipt for a registered letter. The date was still clear, but the name of the person to whom the letter had been addressed was illegible. The creases of the paper and a certain dampness, as if it had been inadvertently touched by a wet finger, had smeared the writing. But the letter had been sent the day before the death of John Siders, and it had been registered from the main post office in G— . This was sufficient for Muller. Then he turned to the desk. Here also there was nothing that could help him. But a sudden thought, came to him, and he took up the blotting pad. This, to his delight, was in the form of a book with a handsome embroidered cover. It looked comparatively new and was, as Muller surmised, a gift from Miss Roemer to her betrothed. But few of the pages had been used, and on two of them a closely written letter had been blotted several times, showing that there had been several sheets of the letter. Muller held it up to the looking-glass, but the repeated blotting had blurred the writing to such an extent that it was impossible to decipher any but a few disconnected words, which gave no clue. On a page further along on the blotter, however, he saw what appeared to be the impression of an address. He held it up to the glass and gave a whistle of delight. The words could be plainly deciphered here:

"MR. LEO PERNBURG,

"FRANKFURT AM MAIN,

"MAINZER LANDSTRASSE."

and above the name was a smear which, after a little study, could be deciphered as the written word "Registered."

With this page of the blotter carefully tucked away in his pocketbook, Muller hurried to the post office, arriving just at closing hour. He made himself known at once to the postmaster, and asked to be shown the records of registered letters sent on a certain date. Here he found scheduled a letter addressed to Mr. Leo Pernburg, Frankfurt am Main, sent by John Siders, G— , Josef Street 7.

Muller then hastened to the telegraph office and despatched a lengthy telegram to the postal authorities in Frankfurt am Main. When the answer came to him next morning, he packed his grip and took the first express train leaving G— . He first made a short visit, however, to Albert Graumann's cell in the prison. Muller was much too kind-hearted not to relieve the anxiety of this man, to whom such mental strain might easily prove fatal. He told Graumann that he was going in search of evidence which might throw light on the death of Siders, and comforted the prisoner with the assurance that he, Muller, believed Graumann innocent, and believed also that within a day or two he would return to G— with proofs that his belief was the right one.

Three days later Muller returned to Grunau and went at once to the Graumann home. It was quite late when he arrived, but he had already notified Miss Roemer by telegram as to his coming, with a request that she should be ready to see him. He found her waiting for him, pale and anxious-eyed, when he arrived. "I have been to Frankfurt am Main," he said, "and I have seen Mr. Pernburg — "

"Yes, yes, that is the name; now I remember," interrupted the girl eagerly. "That is the name of John's friend there."

"I have seen Mr. Pernburg and he gave me this letter." Muller laid a thick envelope on the girl's lap.

She looked down at it, her eyes widening as if she had seen a ghost. "That — that is John's writing," she exclaimed in a hoarse whisper. "Where did it come from?"

"Pernburg gave it to me. The day before his death John Siders sent him this letter, requesting that Pernburg forward it to you before a certain date. When I explained the circumstances to Mr. Pernburg, he gave me the letter at once. I feel that this paper holds the clue to the mystery. Will you open it?"

With trembling hands the girl tore open the envelope. It enclosed still another sealed envelope, without an address. But there was a sheet of paper around this letter, on which was written the following:

My beloved Eleonore:

Before you read what I have to say to you here I want you to promise me, in memory of our love and by your hope of future salvation, that you will do what I ask you to do.

I ask you to give the enclosed letter, although it is addressed to you, to the Judge who will preside in the trial against Graumann. The letter is written to you and will be given back to you. For you, the beloved of my soul, you are the only human being with whom I can still communicate, to whom I can still express my wishes. But you must not give the letter to the Judge until you have assured yourself that the prosecuting attorney insists upon Graumann's guilt. In case he is acquitted, which I do not think probable, then open this letter in the presence of Graumann himself and one or two witnesses. For I wish Graumann, who is innocent, to be able to prove his innocence.

You will know by this time that I have determined to end my life by my own hand. Forgive me, beloved. I cannot live on without you — without the honour of which I was robbed so unjustly.

God bless you.

One who will love you even beyond the grave, Remember your promise. It was given to the dead.

JOHN.

"Oh, what does it all mean?" asked Eleonora, dropping the letter in her lap.

"It is as I thought," replied Muller. "John Siders took his own life, but made every arrangement to have suspicion fall upon Graumann."

"But why? oh, why?"

"It was a terrible revenge. But perhaps — perhaps it was just retribution. Graumaun would not understand that Siders could have been suspected of, and imprisoned for, a theft he had not committed. He must know now that it is quite possible for a man to be in danger of sentence of death even, for a crime of which he is innocent."

"Oh, my God! It is terrible." The girl's head fell across her folded arms on the table. Deep shuddering sobs shook her frame.

Muller waited quietly until the first shock had passed. Finally her sobs died away and she raised her head again. "What am I to do?" she asked.

"You must open this letter to-morrow in the presence of the Police Commissioner and Graumaun."

"But this promise? This promise that he asks of me — that I should wait until the trial?"

"You have not given this promise. Would you take it upon yourself to endanger your guardian's life still more? Every further day spent in his prison, in this anxiety, might be fatal."

"But this promise? The promise demanded of me by the man to whom I had given my love? Is it not my duty to keep it?"

Muller rose from his chair. His slight figure seemed to grow taller, and the gentleness in his voice gave way to a commanding tone of firm decision.

"Our duty is to the living, not to the dead. The dead have no right to drag down others after them. Believe me, Miss Roemer, the purpose that was in your betrothed's mind when he ended his own life, has been fulfilled. Albert Graumann knows now what are the feelings of a man who bears the prison stigma unjustly. He will never again judge his fellow-men as harshly as he has done until now. His soul has been purged in these terrible days; have you the right to endanger his life needlessly?"

"Oh, I do not know! I do not know what to do."

"I have no choice," said Muller firmly. "It is my duty to make known the fact to the Police Commissioner that there is such a letter in existence. The Police Commissioner will then have to follow his duty in demanding the letter from you. Mr. Pernburg, Sider's friend, saw this argument at once. Although he also had a letter from the dead man, asking him to send the enclosure to you, registered, on a certain date, he knew that it was his duty to give all the papers to the authorities. Would it not be better for you to give them up of your own free will?" Muller took a step nearer the girl and whispered: "And would it not be a noble revenge on your part? You would be indeed returning good for evil."

Eleonora clasped her hands and her lips moved as if in silent prayer. Then she rose slowly and held out the letters to Muller. "Do what you will with them," she said. "My strength is at an end."

The next day, in the presence of Commissioner Lange and of the accused Albert Graumann, Muller opened the letter which he had received from Miss Roemer and read it aloud. The girl herself, by her own request, was not present. Both Muller and Graumann understood that the strain of this message from the dead would be too much for her to bear. This was the letter:

G— , September 21st.

My beloved:

When you put this letter in the hands of the Judge, I will have found in death the peace that I could never find on earth. There was no chance of happiness for me since I have realised that I love you, that you love me, and that I must give you up if I am to remain what I have always been — in spite of everything— a man of honour.

Albert Graumann would keep his word, this I know. Wherever you might follow me as my wife, there his will would have been before us, blasting my reputation, blackening the flame which you were to bear.

I could not have endured it. My soul was sick of all this secrecy, sick at the injustice of mankind. In spite of worldly success, my life was cold and barren in the strange land to which I had fled. My home called to me and I came back to it.

I kissed the earth of my own country, and I wept at my mother's grave. I was happy again under the skies which had domed above my childhood. For I am an honest man, beloved, and I always have been.

One day I sat at table beside the man — the Judge who condemned me, here in G— in those terrible days. He naturally did not know me again. I, myself, brought the conversation around to a professional subject. I asked him if it were not possible that circumstantial evidence could lie; if the entire past, the reputation of the accused would not be a factor in his favour. The Judge denied it. It was his opinion, beyond a doubt, that circumstantial evidence was sufficient to convict anyone.

My soul rose within me. This infallibility, this legal arrogance, aroused my blood. "That man should have a lesson!" I said to myself.

But I had forgotten it all — all my anger, all

my hatred and bitterness, when I met you. I dare not trust myself to think of you too much, now that everything is arranged for the one last step. It takes all my control to keep my decision unwavering while I sit here and tell you how much your love, your great tenderness, your sweet trust in me, meant to me.

Let me talk rather of Albert Graumann. I will forgive him for believing in my guilt, but I cannot forgive him that he, the man of cultivation and mental grasp, could not believe it possible for a convicted thief to have repented and to have lived an honest life after the atonement of his crime. I still cannot believe that this was Graumann's opinion. I am forced to think that it was an excuse only on his part, an excuse to keep us apart, an excuse to keep you for himself.

You are lost to me now. There is nothing more in life for me. If the injustice of mankind has stained my honour beyond repair, has robbed me of every chance of happiness at any time and in any place, then I die easily, beloved, for there is little charm in such a life as would be mine after this.

But I do not wish to die quite in vain. There are two men who have touched my life, who need the lesson my death can teach them. These men are Albert Graumann and the prosecuting attorney Gustav Schmidt, the man who once condemned me so cruelly. His present position would make him the representative of the state in a murder trial, and I know his opinions too well not to foresee that he would declare Graumann guilty because of the circumstantial evidence which will be against him. My letter, given to the Presiding Judge after the Attorney has made his speech, will cause him humiliation, will ruin his brilliant arguments and cast ridicule upon him.

Do not think me hard or revengeful. I do not hate anyone now that death is so near. But is it inhuman that I should want to teach these two men a lesson? a lesson which they need, believe me, and it is such a slight compensation for the torture these last eight years have been to me!

And now I will explain in detail all the circumstances. I have arranged that Albert Graumann shall come to me on the evening of September 23rd between 7 and 8 o'clock. I asked him to do so by letter, asking him also to keep the fact of his visit to me a secret. To-night, the 22nd of September, I received his answer promising that he would come. Therefore I can look upon everything that is to happen, as having already happened, for now there need be no further change in my plans. I will send this letter this evening to my friend Pernburg in Frankfurt am Main. In case anything should happen that would render impossible for me to carry out my plans, I will send Pernburg another letter asking him not to carry out the instructions of the first.

I can now proceed to tell you what will happen here to-morrow evening, the 23rd of September.

Albert Graumann will come to me, unknown to his family or friends, as I have asked him to come. I will so arrange it that the old servant will see him come in but will not see him go out. My landlady will not be in my way, for she has already told me that she will spend the night of the 23rd with her mother, in another part of the city. It is to be a birthday celebration I believe, so that I can be certain her plans will not be changed.

Graumann and I will be alone, therefore, with no reliable witnesses near. I will keep him there for a little while with commonplace conversation, for I have nothing to say to him. If he moves near the desk I will upset the inkbottle. The spots on his clothes will be another evidence against him. I will endeavour to get him to keep my jewelry which is, as you know, of considerable value. I will tell him that I am going away for a while and ask him to take charge of it for me. I, myself, will take him down to the door and let him out, when I have satisfied myself that the old servant is in bed or at least at the back of the house. The revolver which shall end my misery is Graumann's property. I took it from its place without his knowledge.

The 10,000 gulden which I told my landlady were still in the house, and which would therefore be thought missing after my death, I have deposited in a bank in Frankfort in your name. Here is the certificate of deposit.

I will endeavour not to hold the revolver sufficiently close to have the powder burn my clothes. And I will exert every effort of mind and body to throw it far from me after I have fired the fatal shot. I think that I will be able to do this, for I am a very good shot and I have no fear of death. One thing more I will do, to turn aside all suspicion of suicide. I will write a letter to some person who does not exist, a letter which will make it appear as if I were in excellent humour and planning for the future.

And now, good-bye to life. People have called me eccentric, they may be right. This last deed of mine at least, is out of the ordinary. No one will say now that ended my life in a moment of darkened mind, in a rush of despair. My brain is perfectly clear, my heart beats calmly, now that I have arranged everything for my departure from this world of falsehood and unreality. My last deed shall go to prove to the world how little actual, apparent facts can be trusted.

The one thing real, the one thing true in all this world of falsehood was your love and your trust. I thank you for it.

> THEODOR BELLMANN,
> known as
> JOHN SIDERS.

Joseph Muller refuses to take any particular credit for this case. The letter would have come in time to prevent Graumann's conviction without his assistance, he says. The only person whose gratitude he has a right to is Prosecuting Attorney Gustav Schmidt. He managed to have the Police Commissioner in G— read the letter in detail to the attorney. But Muller himself knows that it failed of its effect, so far as that dignitary was concerned. For nothing but open ridicule could ever convince a man of such decided opinions that he is not the one infallible person in the world.

But Albert Graumann had learned his lesson. And he told Muller himself that the few days of life which might remain to him were a gift to him from the detective. He felt that his weak heart would not have stood the strain and the disgrace of an open trial, even if that trial ended in acquittal. Two months later he was found dead in his bed, a calm smile on his lips.

Before he died he had learned that it was the undaunted courage of his timid little old aunt that had brought Muller to take charge of the case and to free her beloved nephew from the dreaded prison. And the last days that these two passed together were very happy.

But as aforesaid, Muller refuses to have this case included in the list of his successes. He did not change the ultimate result, he merely anticipated it, he says.